Bella Sara™

5

Fiery Fiona

HarperCollins®, ☰®, and Harper Festival®
are trademarks of HarperCollins Publishers.

Bella Sara: Fiery Fiona
Artwork by Jennifer L. Meyer
© Hidden City Games, Inc. © 2005–2009 conceptcard. All rights reserved.
BELLA SARA is a trademark of conceptcard and is used by Hidden City Games under license.
Licensed by Granada Ventures Limited.
Printed in the United States of America. All rights reserved.

For information address HarperCollins Children's Books,
a division of HarperCollins Publishers,
1350 Avenue of the Americas, New York, NY 10019.
www.harpercollinschildrens.com
www.bellasara.com

Library of Congress catalog card number: 2008939056
ISBN 978-0-06-167333-7
❖
First Edition

Bella Sara™

5

Fiery Fiona

Written by Felicity Brown
Illustrated by Jennifer L. Meyer

HarperFestival®
A Division of HarperCollinsPublishers

Mr. Parson

1

"And then the fiery red mare, Fiona, galloped off through the forest, her silky mane and tail streaming behind her like flames in the wind." Twelve-year-old Astrid Sundlo closed her eyes, imagining the scene just as she'd pictured it so many times before. "The brave girl with the blond braids sat astride the horse's glossy back, riding as naturally as if she'd been born there. Finally, the glorious fire horse left the forest and galloped into the castle courtyard. Cheering filled the air as the citizens of the land

gathered to honor the courage of the pair in saving the Rose Dragons from drowning and returning them safely to their home."

"Is that finally the end?" Astrid's younger brother, Tondy, complained. "Because I'm tired of hearing about Fiona. I want another story about the Nix."

Astrid's eyes flew open. The cheers of the adoring crowd faded. She found herself once more where she always was—in Canter Hollow, the small, sleepy village in the shadow of Rolandsgaard Castle at Trails End, the ancient estate that lay at the center of the land of North of North. She and Tondy were sitting in the hot afternoon sun on the edge of the fountain in the town square. They were waiting for their mother to finish delivering her latest batch of fresh-baked bread and pies to the grocer's shop.

Astrid glanced up at the marble horse statue rising from the center of the fountain, and from there even farther up to the majestic castle that towered over the town in the distance. Its upper terraces seemed to tremble in the thick haze that hung over the valley. For a moment, it had felt as if Astrid were truly that girl in her story, having adventures, living an exciting life like the heroes of the old legends, loved by the horses she so adored. . . .

But now here she was again, back in her regular, boring old life, with hardly a horse around. She glanced over toward the only equine in sight, a stout little Root Pony grazing in a patch of shade. Astrid's gaze lingered on the pony, just as it always did on any equine she encountered, from old Mr. Vibbard's swaybacked dappled-gray mare to the luminescent-green Dynasty horse who lived at the edge of Darkcomb Forest. Whatever shape, size, or color they may be, Astrid loved them all. Her bedroom was papered in sketches of horses, and although she normally had little enthusiasm for helping her mother with her baking business, she always volunteered to grate the carrots and apples when Mrs. Sundlo was asked to make a birthday cake for a horse.

"Astrid?" Tondy leaned closer and splashed her. The water was ice-cold against Astrid's sun-warmed skin. "Hey, wake up and stop dreaming!"

Astrid frowned at her brother. Why was everyone always telling her to stop dreaming? What harm was there in dreams?

"I'm not dreaming," she told him. "I'm just doing what Mother told me to do—keeping you entertained so you don't wander off and fall in the lake."

Tondy scowled back at her. "Then entertain me," he demanded. "Tell me a *good* story. A Nix story!"

"You really want to hear about the Nix *again*?" Astrid glanced toward the grocer's shop, wondering when her mother would emerge. "It's way too hot for that! Besides, every time I tell you a Nix story you end up keeping the whole house awake with your nightmares."

"Nix! Nix!" Tondy chanted stubbornly.

Astrid sighed, blowing a strand of straw-blond hair off her sweaty forehead.

"Fine," she said. "Um, there once was a little boy named Tondy. One night he fell asleep in the kitchen when he was supposed to be sifting the flour for his mother's baking. But he awoke when he felt something scampering across his legs. A moment later he screamed, for his clothes were on fire! It was then that he knew the Nix Darkling had been there. He could never sleep in the same room with any sort of fire ever again. The end."

Tondy frowned, not seeming pleased. "That was too short," he said. "Anyway, you left out a bunch of important details, like how you can keep the

Nix away by throwing the last bite of your supper into the flames. Don't forget, the Nix is a real creature of fire, not like Fiona."

"Fiona is real," Astrid protested, not bothering to argue the first part. After all, she too had believed in the Nix when she was Tondy's age. Their older brothers, Valto and Kimo, had seen to that. They'd tried to spook her with the legend of the mysterious creature that haunted hearths and fire pits, causing mayhem everywhere it went. "Fiona is one of the four great horses of legend who met as foals at the hundredth anniversary celebration of the forming of the Valkyrie Sisterhood."

"Maybe." Tondy shrugged, little impressed. "But it doesn't matter. You'll never meet her. A legendary horse isn't going to show up in boring old Canter Hollow. But the Nix could be anywhere! Valto says that wherever there is fire, you might find the Nix." He shivered despite the heat, wrapping his small arms around himself. "Tell me a better Nix story!"

"Later." Astrid had just spotted the town's blacksmith striding across the town square toward his forge. "Mr. Smithin!" she called out, waving. "Are you shoeing any horses today?"

The man turned toward them, shading his eyes against the sun. "Well, hello there, Sundlos," he called out in his booming voice, his broad, ruddy face breaking into a smile. "And yes, Astrid. It so happens I'm on my way back to the forge to meet a pair of winged horses from the Skyloft estate." He shook his head. "I only hope I can get the forge hot enough. It hasn't been burning quite as well as it used to, ever since I came back from my vacation."

"I could help you if you like," Astrid suggested eagerly, jumping to her feet. She loved assisting at the forge when the blacksmith worked on the local horses' feet. Suddenly remembering her babysitting duties, she added, "Er, I mean, *we* could help. Come on, Tondy."

She tugged at her brother's arm, but Tondy yanked it free. "Mother told us to stay here," he said. "Besides, it's too hot to go near the forge."

Mr. Smithin laughed. "Aye, that it is, son," he agreed. "You've got a smart fellow there, Astrid!"

Before Astrid could argue—or try to talk Tondy into changing his mind—her mother emerged from the grocer's shop just across the square. Mrs. Sundlo's round face was dotted with sweat, and her blond bun looked wilted in the heat.

"Well, hello, Mr. Smithin," she greeted the blacksmith as she hurried over. "Hot enough for you?"

Mr. Smithin tipped his well-worn hat to her. "Indeed. A summer shower is what we need to clear the air."

"Be careful what you wish for," Mrs. Sundlo said, shaking her head. "Remember the spring rains." Heavy downpours a month earlier had caused a series of mudslides up in the mountains near by.

"Mother, Mr. Smithin says he could use my help at the forge," Astrid broke in. "May I go? Please?"

"Only if you can spare her, of course," Mr. Smithin added.

"Another time would be better." Astrid's mother bent to retrieve her cake boxes. "I'm afraid I need the children to help me deliver the rest of these pies and cakes before suppertime."

Astrid bit her lip, knowing better than to argue with her mother. "Sorry, Mr. Smithin," she said. "Maybe tomorrow?"

Once again her mother shook her head. "Tomorrow I need you to carry a couple of pies to your grandfather, remember?"

"Going up the mountain, eh?" Mr. Smithin said. "That sounds like a fine errand for a summer day. Tell Nikolas

I said hello, will you, Astrid?"

"I promise." Astrid was still disappointed that she wouldn't get to watch Mr. Smithin work on the winged horses' hooves. But at least she could look forward to visiting her grandfather and his ancient, loyal Fjord horse, Paal, the next day.

Perhaps Paal will take me for a ride, she thought, as she followed her mother and Tondy across the square. *It may not be the same as riding Fiona, but it's certainly better than nothing.*

2

The next morning dawned just as hot and still as the previous one. By the time she joined her parents and three brothers at the table for breakfast, Astrid was already coated in a thin sheen of perspiration. "The fire seems hotter than ever today!" Astrid grumbled, mopping her brow with a scratchy homespun napkin.

Her mother shot an uncertain glance toward the crackling, spitting fire. "Odd you should say so," she murmured. "In fact, it does seem hotter than usual lately. I've actually had to adjust my baking times."

"Uh-oh." Tondy's eyes grew wide. "I bet it's the Nix!"

Astrid rolled her eyes. "See? I told you two you shouldn't tell him so many tall tales," she told her older brothers. "He'll be seeing the Nix in the candles in his room next."

Kimo chortled and speared another sausage with his fork. "Hey, Tondy," he said. "Remind me to tell you sometime about the Nix's tiny cousin, the candle-Nix."

"Enough, boys," Mr. Sundlo said sternly. He glanced toward Astrid as he helped himself to butter for his biscuit. "You'd better set out early for Father's cabin, Astrid. It looks to be another scorcher, although Mrs. Jorma's Cloud-skipper predicts we might finally get some rain soon."

"Rain?" Astrid's eldest brother, Valto, who was as tall and lanky and fair as Kimo was short and stocky and dark, cast a skeptical glance out the window. "Sky looks dry as a bone to me."

"Oh, really?" Astrid challenged him, irritated by his know-it-all tone. "Didn't you hear Father say Cloudskipper predicted rain? I suppose you know more than a Stratus horse about what the clouds might bring?"

"What clouds?" Kimo retorted. He was always up for an argument. "I don't see any clouds, do you?"

Normally Astrid was more than ready to put Kimo in his place, but today she wasn't in the mood. "Forget it," she muttered, turning her attention to her breakfast. She found herself eating faster than usual, looking forward to the cooler, lighter air high up on the slopes of Mount Whitemantle.

Half an hour later Astrid was free of her brothers and was plodding up the trail leading through the foothills. The

box of pies and bread her mother had packed was awkward to carry. Astrid had to shift it from one arm to the other. She tried to distract herself by looking at the uprooted trees and other damage done by the recent mudslides.

If only I had a horse to ride, this journey would be much easier, she thought with a sigh as she climbed over a fallen tree trunk. *It would also be much more fun!*

She crested a wooded hillock that had been blocking the view ahead, and suddenly the glorious expanse of Mount Whitemantle stood before her. As always, Astrid's gaze went first to the massive twin horsehead statues known as the Bookends. Carved out of the mountain itself, the sculptures depicted Bella and Bello, the legendary leaders of all magical horses in North of North. *It would be so amazing to ride Bella,* she thought, studying the strong, elegant lines of the enormous chiseled heads. Walking the wind, having incredible adventures, just like Bella did with the child goddess Sara . . . but Fiona, with the mane and tail that matched her fiery spirit, was still Astrid's favorite.

Astrid was so caught up in staring at the Bookends that she forgot to watch where she was going. She tripped over a loose stone on the trail, lurched forward, and nearly dropped her package. Managing to find her feet just in time, she heaved a sigh of relief.

"Stop dreaming, Astrid," she whispered, mocking what she knew her family would say. "Pay attention to real life instead of your imaginary adventures."

At least for one day she wouldn't have to hear such things, for her grandfather would never say them. He was the only one who didn't seem to think she was wrong to dream.

Nikolas Sundlo made rustic furniture and hand-carved animals out of the trees that blanketed the slopes of Mount Whitemantle, where he lived in a cabin that he had built with his own hands. Astrid loved visiting him. Even the long trek up to his cabin was part of the pleasure. The towering trees and endless views always set Astrid's imagination soaring.

Or at least they did when the weather was less oppressive. This time Astrid could think only of reaching her destination and having a cool drink of water from her grandfather's spring.

Reminded of the weather, she glanced up at the sky. To her surprise, she saw storm clouds gathering on the horizon.

"Hah!" she said, pleased. Thinking of Kimo and Valto being proved wrong gave Astrid a burst of energy, and her mind and muscles hummed as she hiked up the steep, rocky trail.

After an hour she stopped to rest in a meadow, pulling out the apple she'd brought as a snack. The clouds were beginning to roll closer, and as she squinted up at them, Astrid caught a flash of movement immediately overhead. It was a winged horse—a Starjumper, by the looks of it—swooping along on some business of its own.

As she watched the horse soar overhead, its glittering wings flapping against the air currents, Astrid felt her heart fill with longing. What must it be like to fly that way? She wished she knew a winged horse well enough to beg a ride and find out. The only horses she knew well enough to ride at all were the ancient Paal and her neighbor Kaia's horse friend, a Glittermane mare named Sparkle. Astrid had enjoyed several rides on the kindhearted Sparkle, although she had never had the courage to approach Kaia's father's massive Redwood Draft, Dax, or Kaia's mother's pretty rainbow mare, Arca. If only Astrid's own family had the means to care for a horse.

"Ah, well," she murmured, as the Starjumper swooped out of sight. It was pointless to dwell on such matters.

As Astrid stepped back onto the familiar trail, she noticed yet another change in the landscape since her last trip up the mountain. This time it was a huge boulder that had slipped several yards down a steep slope, carried on a mud-slide.

"Is that a cave?" Astrid whispered to herself, spying an opening in the earth where the boulder had once stood. She set down the box of baked goods and climbed up the slope for a better look.

To her disappointment, there was no cave—only a sort of sinkhole. As she was about to turn away, she noticed something wedged into the bottom. She picked her way carefully down into the hole and reached for the package. It was wrapped in leather and surprisingly heavy.

Interesting, she thought, leaning forward and grasping the edge of the muddy leather with both hands. Maybe it was some sort of long lost treasure, hidden here by a magical gemdigger dog. Or even something better—like the shield of a Valkyrie!

She yanked the mysterious package loose and set it on the dry ground at the edge of the hole. Its rope bindings were old and frayed, and Astrid's fingers quickly worked the knots loose until the bundle fell open. To her disappointment, however, all it contained was a jumble of old, dusty-looking tools—a heavy hammer, a dented chisel, and a few other items.

"Stonecutter's tools," she murmured, picking up a chisel and examining it.

The tools looked old. Not just old—*ancient*. Deciding that her grandfather might like to see them, Astrid gathered them up again in their leather wrapping. Then she turned to pick her way back down to the trail—just in time to spy her box of pies and bread shuffling off toward a bush as if it had sprouted legs!

"Hey!" Astrid cried, dropping the heavy package and rushing to grab the box.

When she lifted it, she revealed a sheepish-looking little animal with ash-gray fur and a long, full tail that resembled the silky tassel at the top of a corncob. A tassel mouse! The tiny creature was panting with the effort of dragging the box. He stared up at Astrid for a second, and then disappeared into the bushes with a flick of his tail.

"Wait!" Astrid called after him. "I'm sorry, I didn't mean to scare you. Please come back!"

Opening the box, she pinched a crumb off one of the loaves, knowing her grandfather wouldn't mind. She set the crumb in the middle of the path, and then stepped back and waited.

The tassel mouse couldn't resist. He peeked out, nose and whiskers twitching. Then he darted out, grabbed the crumb, and raced away again.

Astrid gave chase, following him through the bushes and up a short slope. "It's okay!" she called after him. "Please don't run away. I want to—*whoops!*"

She skidded to a stop just in time to keep herself from tumbling into a deep crevice in the rock. When she looked down, startled by the close call, she saw the tassel mouse clinging to the edge of the drop-off with his tiny front paws, his hind legs pumping helplessly in midair.

"Hang on!" Astrid exclaimed.

Dropping to her knees, she reached down and scooped him into her hands, lifting him to safety. She set him on a nearby rock where he sat trembling, his whiskers flicking anxiously. "There you go," Astrid said. "That was a close one!"

The tassel mouse chittered at her gratefully. Then he jumped from the rock to her knee, scampering quickly up her shirt to perch on her shoulder.

Astrid smiled. Okay, a tassel mouse wasn't a horse. But it was still nice to have a new friend!

"Aren't you sweet!" she exclaimed, reaching up carefully to stroke the little creature's soft fur. "And you're no bigger than the cork in the cider jug back home." She chuckled. "Maybe that's what I should call you—Cork!"

The little creature chittered agreeably, wriggling his whiskers. He seemed pleased with his new name.

"Nice to meet you, Cork. I'm Astrid," Astrid said. "Now then, I wonder where this crack came from. I've climbed up this way to pick berries lots of times and never saw it before. The mudslides must have created it, I guess. Oh, but wait! Is that . . . a cave?"

She peered over the edge of the crevice. Sure enough, there was an opening in the rock just below the lip.

"What do you say, Cork? Feel like a little adventure?" Astrid asked, her heart beating faster. How many myths and legends had she heard that involved the deep, dark reaches of mysterious caves? She even had a sketch on her wall back home of herself riding Fiona into a dark cave in search of the rarely seen translucent Lithohorse.

Cork clung to Astrid's shirt as she climbed over the lip and lowered herself into the opening. The clouds were looming closer, blocking some of the sun's rays, but there was enough light to see a few yards into the cave.

"I think I see light at the far end."

Astrid squinted into the darkness. "It's not really a cave—it seems to be more of a tunnel."

She hurried forward into the darkness, keeping one hand on the rough stone wall and both eyes on the speck of light at the far end. The passage was longer than she expected. Finally, she emerged into a sort of hollow surrounded by high, sheer stone walls. It was dim and damp, the stone floor coated with moss and most of the sunlight blocked by shadows. When she looked up, Astrid saw the immense stone image of Bello looming directly above. Across from her, half hidden in shadow, was a massive stone door. Where could it lead?

"By Sigga's sword!" Astrid exclaimed. "No one can possibly even know this place exists. Until that passage was opened up by the mudslides, it was totally hidden from the rest of the world!"

Astrid knew as many old stories and legends as just about anyone in

North of North, and she had never heard of this magical spot at the base of Bello's monument.

She moved closer to the door for a better look. The carved images of horses capered around the bottom edge, thick with dust but nonetheless seeming almost alive. One particular horse near the top stood out among them all. That one—could it be?

"Fiona," she murmured in awe, stretching on her tiptoes so that her fingers could trace the carving of a beautiful mare with a long mane and tail that flowed behind her like fire. "I'd know you anywhere."

Astrid next examined the orchid carved in the center of the door. The lettering above and below it was like nothing she'd seen before. The door itself was just as mysterious; she could see no handle nor any other way of opening it. She pushed against it with all her strength, but she might as well have been

pushing against the mountain itself for all the difference she made.

"What do you think, Cork? What does all this mean?"

The little mouse merely chirped uncertainly. Then he scurried along her shoulder blade, clinging to her shirt with his tiny claws, and disappeared into her pocket. A moment later his head popped out, his cheeks bulging with the crumbs he'd found inside.

Astrid smiled distractedly, still focused on the mysterious door. Where did it lead? How did you open it? Could it have stood hidden here since long ago—perhaps even from the time of the Valkyries? Her mind raced with dozens of questions. Perhaps her grandfather would have some ideas. . . .

That reminded her that she was still a long way from her grandfather's cozy cabin. Peering up past the Bello monument toward the sun, she realized the clouds were much thicker now.

"Come on, Cork," she said reluctantly. "We'd better go. It could rain soon, and we don't want to be caught in another mudslide. Maybe we can come back here another day."

Once back on the trail, she retrieved her box of baked goods and the old tools she'd found and continued on her way with Cork in her pocket.

Finally, she reached her grandfather's cabin. A sturdy dwelling made from logs with the bark still attached, it was nestled into the base of a giant evergreen, seeming to have sprouted there out of the great tree's roots. Her grandfather was in the front yard, filling a bucket with cold water from a nearby stream. He was as wrinkled and brown as the bark of a tree, with gnarled hands and a crown of white hair. His Fjord horse companion, Paal, grazed nearby with several small birds perched on his swayed old back.

"Well, what a pleasant surprise," Nikolas greeted Astrid cheerfully. "I've been wondering when you would come to see me again."

Astrid hop scotched across the stream and followed him into the cabin, with Cork chittering in her pocket. "I have something for you, Granddad," she said. "Two things, actually."

She handed him the box of baked goods, hardly allowing him time to inhale its delectable scent before she pulled out the tools she'd found. Her words tumbled over one another as she told him of all her adventures that day.

"Lovely to meet you, Cork," Nikolas said. He bowed his head toward the little mouse, who chirped shyly in response.

"So what do you think, Granddad?" Astrid asked eagerly.

"About what, exactly?" he asked, smiling. "You've told me so much!"

She laughed. "First, the tools. Are these stonecutter's tools?"

He picked up the chisel and

weighed it in his hands. "Indeed they are. Made of durium, no less—that's a metal one doesn't see often these days. And they look very old indeed. You found them under a rock, eh?" He frowned thoughtfully.

"A rock that led me to that secret door under the Bookends. I wonder if they're connected," Astrid said. Her eagerness welled up again. "I wonder if the same person who carved the Bookends carved the door. I wonder if—"

Nikolas held up his hand for silence. They both listened as thunder rumbled faintly.

"Will you stay here with Paal and me tonight, or does your mother need you back?" he asked.

"She needs me back," Astrid said reluctantly. "Lots of breads and pies to deliver."

"Well, then, I'm sorry to say that I think you'd best be off," Nikolas told her. "That storm is on its way. I don't want you getting caught on the mountain when the rain starts. My old bones tell me we haven't seen our last mudslide this year."

Astrid was disappointed, but she knew her grandfather was never wrong about the weather. He was nearly as accurate as a Stratus horse! "All right," she said. She poked at the tools with one foot. "Want to keep these, Granddad?"

He smiled. "What do I need with stonecutter's tools?" He reached over to ruffle her hair. "I have spent my life working with wood. I don't plan to change now."

Astrid bundled the tools up again. Then she went outside to feed Paal the sugar cookies she'd brought him.

"I thought you'd like these," she said, scratching him at the base of his brushlike mane. "Much easier to chew than carrots!"

Paal gobbled the cookies and then nudged at her, looking for more. When his muzzle bumped against her shirt pocket, Cork let out a startled squawk. Paal lifted his head, glaring at the mouse in surprise.

Astrid laughed. "Be nice, you two!" she said, giving both horse and mouse a quick pat. "I'll see you again soon, Paal. Maybe next time we can go for a ride, okay?"

The Fjord horse cocked an ear agreeably and then went back to grazing. Astrid turned away, wishing there were time for a quick ride. True, all Paal ever did was plod around at a pace slower than she could walk on her own two feet. Even so, just being on a horse—a *real* horse, in real life, not just in her imagination— was her favorite feeling in the world.

But one glance at her grandfather's anxious face told her it was out of the question. Bidding him farewell, she hurried back to the trail home.

Astrid headed straight down the mountain and didn't dawdle, not even to pick flowers or explore the trees uprooted by the mudslides. Even so, she was only halfway down when the first drops of rain spattered onto the dry dirt around her. A moment after that came the sizzle of lightning—and a loud crack as it struck something very close by!

CHAPTER

4

*C*ork let out a squeak of alarm. "It's all right," Astrid said, her heart pounding. She wasn't afraid of much, but she hated lightning.

Glancing around as the rain increased into a steady downpour and thunder boomed, she realized she was almost at the spot where she'd discovered the tunnel. She raced forward through the driving rain, one hand over her pocket to offer Cork what little shelter she could. It was a frightening climb over the slick, wet rock and through the wind-whipped brush, but they made it into the dry passageway.

Inside, the thunder was muffled. Astrid listened to it, her feet automatically taking her through the tunnel to the hollow. When she reached it, she looked out and tried to see the mysterious door, but it was hardly visible through the sheets of rain. However, she could see the other opening in the wall off to one side.

"This storm looks like it won't be moving on anytime soon. We can either stay in here and be bored and dry, or run over to that other tunnel and maybe have something interesting to explore," she told Cork. "What do you think?"

Cork looked uncertain, but Astrid had already made up her mind.

"Hold on!" she cried, plunging back out into the rain.

Seconds later she burst into the second tunnel. The ceiling was a little lower than the other one, but the passage was wider.

"No light at the end of this one," she murmured, peering around the first twist in the tunnel. "I wish I had a candle. . . ."

Cork suddenly popped out of her pocket and scampered up to her shoulder. He tipped his head back, chittering and dancing as he pointed upward.

"What is it?" Astrid asked, tilting her head back.

There on the ceiling were dozens of large, chubby caterpillars pulsing with gentle greenish light.

"Glowworms!" she cried. "That's handy!"

She reached up and carefully peeled one of the glowworms off the ceiling. He was about the size of her index finger, with pale eyes blinking sleepily at her from the ends of his antennae. She stroked him gently with one finger. The little worm wriggled happily, and his greenish glow increased. "Little friend, would you mind lighting our way through this dark tunnel? I'll be sure to return you safely to your family afterward."

The glowworm pulsed brightly. Astrid decided that meant yes.

With the glowworm lighting their way, she and Cork were soon rounding the many twists and turns of the tunnel. Astrid wasn't sure how long they walked before the light increased beyond the glowworm's pale luminosity. They had reached the other end.

The thunder and lightning still raged outside, but the rain had slowed enough to give Astrid a view of a small, sloping valley dotted with large boulders. Wildflowers grew in the grassy swathes among the great boulders. The entire valley was surrounded by high stone walls stretching straight up toward the Bookends. "I always thought I knew this mountain as well as anyone," Astrid told Cork in amazement. "But now it seems—"

The rest of her words were lost in an immense clap of thunder, as loud as if the entire mountain had suddenly been split in two by a giant's sledgehammer. Cork let out a squeak and dived deeper into her pocket as a sudden gust of wind whipped around them. Astrid was about to duck back into the tunnel, but lightning flashed again, this time showing her a glimpse of color peeking out from just beyond one of the largest of the boulders scattered across the valley. That shade of bright indigo could not belong to any wildflower she'd ever seen. . . .

The boulder was only a short distance away. On impulse she set down the glowworm and the bundle of tools, and then dived out into the full force of the storm. She raced toward that flash of color, hoping the lightning wouldn't find her as she ran. She rounded the boulder and stopped short.

She was surrounded by a circle of ancient standing stones. A woman was camped within the circle. She was older than even Astrid's grandfather, with wise aquamarine eyes in a face as brown and wrinkled as a nut. Her expression was kind and welcoming. The indigo color belonged to a large sheet of canvas the woman had stretched over the stones, protecting herself and her campfire from the storm.

"Greetings, young friend," the woman said. "I see the storm caught you unawares. Come and warm yourself by the fire. I am a traveler through these parts. My name is Philenia True."

"I'm Astrid." Astrid was a bit wary—although strange horses often passed through the area, it was rare to meet an unknown human. But when Cork hopped out of her pocket and scurried over to perch at the woman's feet, accepting a small bit of crust from her hand, Astrid relaxed. If Cork trusted this Philenia, surely she meant them no harm.

"The fire feels good," Astrid said, leaning forward to warm her hands. A log tumbled and sparked, making her jump in surprise, and she laughed. "Although my little brother Tondy might not say so," she added. "He would be worried that it's the perfect hiding spot for the Nix!"

Philenia chuckled. "Ah, it is nice to see that the old stories are still circulating. Do you enjoy stories, Astrid?"

"Do I!" To her surprise, Astrid found herself pouring out her heart about her favorite stories, that day's adventures, and more. Philenia listened and nodded, making a comment here and there, and before long, Astrid was telling her how much she longed to have adventures like those of the heroes in the old tales, to meet amazing horses, and to explore all of North of North.

"But everyone is always telling me to stop dreaming," she explained. "To buckle down, be sensible."

"It is sensible to dream," Philenia told her. Taking out a small sketch pad and a bit of charcoal, she began to draw with swift, sure strokes. "Dreams are what allow us to do great things."

Astrid sighed and glanced over her shoulder toward the tunnel. "Today has been the most exciting day of my life so far, and if you think about it, not much has really even happened, except that I explored a couple of tunnels and found that mysterious door."

She felt a poke near her ankle. Cork was standing up on a stone by her feet, looking insulted. Astrid laughed. "And of course, I met a new friend," she said, patting the tassel mouse. "*Two* new friends," she added shyly, glancing up at Philenia.

The old woman's eyes twinkled as she looked up from her sketch pad.

"Adventure can come in many forms, my dear," she remarked.

Astrid thought about that as she stared out into the darkness. Night had fallen while they were talking, she noticed with surprise. The rain had tapered off to a soft drizzle, and the air was cool and pleasant. She knew she should go home. Her parents would be worrying about her.

"I want the regular kind of adventure," she continued anyway. "You know, fighting monsters, saving people and horses from evil sorcerers . . ." She straightened her shoulders. "Like a Valkyrie! I want to have a special partner . . . a wonderful horse . . ." Once again she shot Philenia a look, unsure how the old woman would react to her deepest desire. "A horse like—like Fiona."

To her relief, Philenia didn't laugh. "Yes, I thought you might choose Fiona," she murmured. She bent over her sketch pad, the charcoal flying faster.

Growing curious, Astrid leaned

forward. "What are you sketching?" she asked.

Philenia made a few final marks and then held up the pad so Astrid could see.

Astrid gasped. It was a portrait of Fiona herself! Even though it was merely a charcoal drawing, it pulsed with life. The flames of the campfire cast a vibrant red glow over the picture, making the horse seem to prance and caper. It was far better than anything Astrid could ever draw, and for a moment she couldn't speak as she stared at it, her heart filled with longing.

She was startled by a soft neigh from somewhere in the darkness nearby. Leaping to her feet, she stared around. "What was that?"

Philenia was smiling as she looked toward the sound. "Well, hello," she said, as a horse stepped into the circle of fire-light.

Astrid gasped, and for a moment her heart stopped beating. She recognized that horse. She would have recognized her anywhere.

"Fiona!" she cried.

Fiona was even more beautiful than Astrid could have imagined. Tall, sleek, and regal, the stunning mare had a fiery red coat and a mane that fell nearly to her knees.

"This is Astrid," Philenia told the mare. "She needs to get home. Can you help?"

The horse bowed her shapely head and gazed at Astrid with her dark, liquid eyes. In her mind, Astrid felt the mare's assent and gasped aloud with wonder.

"She—I heard her—I mean, I felt

her—" Astrid babbled in amazement.

Then she swallowed hard, trying to regain control of her senses so as not to appear foolish. That was what horses did, after all—they sent their thoughts and emotions directly to the person with whom they wished to communicate. True, none of the horses Astrid knew had ever bothered to communicate with her in that way. Paal had always managed to make his feelings known through more ordinary means.

Is it always so special? Astrid wondered. *Or does it feel this way because it's Fiona?*

"Come, my dear," Philenia said to Astrid. "It is dark, and your family will be worried. You had better get going."

Astrid felt a little shy about mounting the glorious mare. However, Fiona had already stepped over to stand beside one of the boulders. Before she knew it, Astrid felt her body settling into place as if she'd ridden Fiona many times before.

Once Astrid was seated, Philenia lifted Cork up so he could scamper into the girl's pocket. Then she stepped over to pick up the bundle of old tools.

Astrid was surprised. Hadn't she left the tools back in the mouth of the cave, along with . . . "The glowworm!" she burst out suddenly. "Oh, no! I have to return him to his own end of the tunnel—I promised!"

Fiona sent a picture of Philenia carrying the little glowworm back to his family. "Consider it done," Philenia said. "Your promise has become mine, Astrid, and I will see to it immediately."

"Thank you," Astrid said. "Thank you so much. It was wonderful to meet you."

Philenia smiled. "Likewise, my dear," she said. "Now enjoy the trip home—and hang on! I think you'll find Fiona a livelier ride than your grandfather's elderly pony."

Before Astrid could wonder how

Philenia knew about Paal, she felt the great red horse's muscles gather beneath her. She gasped at the feeling of power in the mare's hindquarters as she sprang into a smooth, effortless trot. Fiona was moving faster than Astrid had ever gone before—faster than she'd believed possible. It was still raining, but somehow the horse seemed to dodge between the raindrops, and Astrid remained dry.

Despite such speed, Astrid found the mare's stride smooth and easy. It was so smooth, in fact, that she couldn't help noticing an occasional bobble, the tiniest hesitation in Fiona's stride. What could it mean? Then she forgot about that as Fiona once again began sending images into her mind. She saw four yearlings frolicking on the shores of Teardrop Lake—a glowing red filly, a doe-eyed flaxen chestnut with a tiny set of wings, a sturdy black colt with a lightning-shaped mark across his hindquarters, and a slender-legged bay filly with a pretty, delicately chiseled

face. The four young horses grazed and played, carefree and happy.

The red filly lifted her head from the grass as a child came into view—a girl, innocent and sweet yet somehow sad. After that, each image came quickly and fluttered away again, like scattering butterflies. A regal white mare. A lotus flower upon the still water. A woman sitting at a loom weaving an intricate tapestry . . .

Astrid's eyes flew open. She stared into the darkness without seeing. She had heard countless stories of the first meeting of the four most renowned horses in North of North. It was said to have taken place at the gathering held many, many years ago to celebrate the hundredth anniversary of the forming of the Valkyrie Sisterhood.

According to the legends, that girl in the images was Sara, the child goddess. The other three yearlings were Nike, Thunder, and Jewel. And the fourth young horse was Fiona herself.

The knowledge that she had been given the gift of meeting the now-grown Fiona, of riding her just as she'd imagined so many times, was so overwhelming that Astrid's eyes filled with tears of joy.

Time passed—minutes or hours, Astrid did not know. Eventually the red mare reached Astrid's home. Despite the late hour, candles burned in all the windows. The storm was over, although the trees still dripped and the grass was wet.

"Astrid!" Her mother rushed out of the house. "You're here! We were so afraid that you'd been caught in the storm. . . ."

Astrid's father and brothers were there, too. Valto and Kimo caught her as she slid down from the horse's back and carried her inside. She tried to tell everyone about her day, but they were all talking at once, scolding, clucking, so that she could barely get a word in.

Besides, she realized, she was

absolutely exhausted. She was vaguely aware of her mother shooing her into her bedroom. Then her head touched the clean white softness of her pillow, and she remembered nothing more.

Astrid was smiling when she woke up the next morning. As soon as she glanced out her window, she remembered why: Fiona! The stunning red mare was grazing just outside. She lifted her head from the lush grass and met Astrid's eye. Although horses could not smile in the way that humans did, Astrid could feel a glow of warmth coming from and surrounding the mare.

She threw on the first clothes she could find and rushed outside, hardly daring to believe it hadn't all been a dream. But no, Fiona was still there, warm and solid and full of life. Before she realized what she was doing, Astrid had thrown her arms around the horse's neck. Fiona didn't seem to mind a bit. She lowered her head and nuzzled at the girl's cheek.

There was a burst of chittering from nearby. When Astrid tore her gaze away from Fiona, she saw Cork coming toward them, his small body staggering beneath the weight of a large carrot.

Astrid laughed. "I guess Cork likes you as much as I do," she told Fiona, as she took the carrot and offered it to the horse. "He must if he's willing to share his food!"

For the rest of the day, Astrid spent every second she could with Fiona, carrying her own lunch outside so they could eat together, lovingly brushing the mare's already glossy coat to a burnished shine. The two of them wandered through the fields and meadows behind the Sundlos' home so that Fiona could select the most delectable grasses to eat. Astrid's mother was busy with her baking, but for once she had enlisted Kimo and Valto to help so that Astrid could have the time free.

Once or twice Astrid thought she

again detected the slight flaw in Fiona's stride that she'd felt the night before. *Maybe it's a loose shoe,* she thought, glancing toward the bright gleam of the horseshoes on Fiona's hooves. *I'll have to ask Mr. Smithin if he can help.*

But for the moment, she was content simply to enjoy the mare's company. She had no idea why Fiona had chosen to befriend her, but she didn't care to question it. She was just glad that she was there.

*A*fter having dinner with her family, Astrid stayed outside with Fiona until the darkness chased her back in. She found Tondy waiting for her to tell him his usual bedtime story.

"I suppose you want to hear about the Nix again," she said, as she settled on the edge of his bed in his tiny bedroom.

Tondy shook his head. "Not today," he said. "I want to hear a story about Fiona."

"Really?" Astrid smiled. It seemed she wasn't the only one in the family who'd been won over by the mare! "Hmm, all right. How about this one: In the days of the Valkyrie Sisterhood, there was a glorious red horse known as Fiona . . ."

"Aaaaaaah!"

Astrid's eyes flew open as a scream yanked her out of a sound sleep. She sat bolt upright. "Tondy?" she blurted out.

Leaping out of bed so fast that the sheets tangled around her ankles and almost tripped her, she raced for the door. The glow of the full moon offered plenty of light as she burst into the hallway, nearly colliding with her parents and older brothers.

They all rushed to Tondy's room, where they found him sitting up in bed, bathed in moonlight. He was babbling wildly.

"What is it?" Astrid cried.

"The Nix!" he sobbed. "The Nix! It came into my bed and tried to set me on fire!"

Valto rolled his eyes. "Should've known," he mumbled sleepily. "He had a nightmare, that's all. Let's go back to bed."

Astrid relaxed. Valto was right. "It's your fault, you know," she told him with a yawn. "You keep scaring him."

"No!" Tondy wailed. "It was really here! It ran right over my legs! See?"

"There, there, dear," Mrs. Sundlo said kindly. "I'll fetch you a cup of water." She hurried off toward the kitchen. The older boys were already turning away as well, but Astrid looked where her younger brother was pointing. She gasped.

There were tiny, red, foot-shaped burn marks on Tondy's bare legs! She bent down swiftly. On the floor beside his bed she saw small, sooty footprints leading out of the room. Each had four clawed toes. "Hey," Kimo said, "does anyone else smell smoke?"

Just then their mother let out a terrified cry from the kitchen: *"Fire!"*

*A*strid raced down the hall with the rest of the family, Cork in tow. They all burst into the kitchen to find the woodpile next to the fireplace ablaze. Before their eyes, the fire sprang up and engulfed the kitchen curtains.

"Hurry!" Valto shouted, leaping into action. "We have to put it out before it burns the whole place down!"

Mr. Sundlo was already grabbing the water jug. "Valto, Astrid, get more water from the well!" he cried. "Kimo, use tea towels to try to beat out the sparks. Tondy, you stay back."

Astrid's heart pounded. She saw a finger of flame spring up from the woodpile to lick at her mother's handmade tablecloth. Another escaped out from the hearth, setting the corner of the rug afire.

Then she spied something else—a shadowy little figure perched on the window ledge, staring at her with glowing red eyes. She gasped. Could it be?

"Astrid! Move!" Kimo yelled, giving her a shove.

That push jarred her out of her stupor. She raced outside and grabbed a bucket. Halfway to the well, she stopped and looked back at the house. Black smoke poured from the kitchen windows, and an orange glow pulsed inside.

She looked at the bucket in her hand. It was so small, and she couldn't even carry it more than half full. *It's no use,* she thought helplessly, her eyes filling with tears made worse by the smoke.

We can't beat that fire.

Then she felt a comforting presence wash over her, chasing away her fear and making even the smoke seem less black and horrible. Looking back, she saw Fiona cantering toward her. The mental images were already coming—Astrid looping several buckets over Fiona's back and riding her down to the pond at the bottom of the yard, where she could fill them to the brim and then bring them back to Astrid's parents and brothers.

"Thank you," Astrid cried, already tying the buckets together with the extra rope that always sat by the well. "Thank you!"

When the buckets were in place, Astrid vaulted onto the mare's back, not needing a mounting block this time. "Where are you going?" Kimo yelled, as he struggled toward the back door with a sloshing bucket of water.

"To get more water!" she called back.

Fiona galloped off before Kimo could respond. She crossed the yard in a flash and leaped into the water without pausing. Astrid grasped the horse's mane tightly, as the cold, spring-fed water splashed up around her. She felt the buckets bump against her bare legs and began pushing them down with one hand, so they could fill properly.

The great red horse seemed to know exactly when it was time to burst out of the water again. She galloped back, spray flying off her coat and turning to steam which swirled around her. Once again, Astrid clung to the horse's mane to keep from slipping off her wet back.

Her parents and brothers were waiting to grab the buckets and dump them into the ones they were holding. "More!" Astrid's father shouted hoarsely, as he spun to race back into the burning house. "Please bring more!"

Horse and girl made three more

trips, bringing back full buckets each time. By their final return, Astrid could no longer see flames through the kitchen windows—only thick black smoke pouring out.

"It's just about out," her mother said breathlessly, as Mr. Sundlo and the boys disappeared inside.

Astrid slid down from the mare's back, so weak with relief that her fingers trembled as she removed the buckets. "Thank goodness," she murmured. Then she leaned against the mare's strong, comforting bulk. "And thank you, Fiona. You saved our home."

It wasn't until the next day that Astrid remembered the shadowy figure she'd seen during the fire. She mentioned it to her father as she helped him carry in more wood to replace what had burned.

"Do you—I mean, the Nix isn't real, is it?" she added uncertainly. "Because I could have sworn—"

He dumped his load of logs and then put an arm around her and squeezed her shoulders. "It's understandable, Astrid," he said. "You'd just woken up, the fire and smoke were swirling all around—it's no wonder you were seeing things."

Astrid bit her lip. She wished she could be as sure as her father. The trouble was, she didn't believe it had been a trick of the smoke, or a lingering remnant of a dream, either. She'd *seen* something there on the windowsill.

But Fiona was waiting for her outside, so she put it out of her mind.

The news of the legendary horse's appearance at the Sundlo homestead had spread quickly through Canter Hollow and the surrounding hamlets. Curious townsfolk stopped by all day long to gawk at the beautiful mare, and Astrid's brothers were practically green with envy.

That afternoon, Astrid's mother asked her to help deliver baked goods around Canter Hollow. Astrid wished she could stay with Fiona instead, but her parents had been so patient with her already that she couldn't say no. She and her mother carried several boxes of pies and bread to homes and businesses in town, and then headed out to her friend Kaia's home. The Olav house was much grander than Astrid's own, nestled into sweeping grounds with plenty of grazing for the three horses that lived with the family.

When Astrid and her mother arrived, Mrs. Olav was riding Arca, a milky-white mare with a flowing mane and tail that sparkled with all the colors of the rainbow. The magnificent creature had never paid much attention to Astrid before, but today she gazed curiously at her with her kaleidoscope eyes. Astrid supposed that even the local horses had heard about the visiting celebrity.

"Come inside," Kaia's mother said, dismounting gracefully. "Kaia will be so pleased to see you, Astrid."

The Sundlos followed her into the house. Astrid had always loved the entrance hall, which had carved wooden sea horses decorating the wall panels.

"Is it true?" Kaia cried, racing toward Astrid and grasping her by both hands. "The famous Fiona—is she really at your house? Did you really ride her?"

Astrid smiled and squeezed her friend's hands. "It's true," she confirmed. "I can't wait to tell you all about it!"

The two girls hurried into the parlor while their mothers carried the baked goods into the kitchen. There was a fire burning high in the tile-lined fireplace, making the room overly warm. Astrid sat down on a settee as far from it as she could. She first introduced Kaia to Cork, and then moved on to describe her adventures.

"It all started when I went up the mountain to visit my granddad," she began.

But Astrid had hardly finished the first part of her tale when a flash of motion near the fire caught her eye. Turning to look, she saw a shadowy form dash out of the fire, leaving sooty footprints behind. It was like a little goblin of ash, with long, skinny dark limbs and flames for hair. The creature leaped onto the windowsill and dived out the open window.

An instant later the long silk curtains began to smolder!

K aia let out a scream. "Fire!" she cried, grabbing a vase of flowers and tossing the water onto the curtain. The flames vanished with a sizzle.

Astrid ran to the door. "It's the Nix! I saw it!" she cried. This time she was determined not to let the destructive little creature get away.

She burst out of the house just in time to see the dark figure race across the lawn, heading toward town. It trailed sparks and bits of flame as it ran, and

Astrid had to stop several times to stomp out little fires that had started in the grass. "Fire! Fire!" Astrid yelled as she dashed past. Answering shouts came as people noticed what was happening.

Astrid lost sight of the Nix as he entered the village. But it was easy to follow the trail of sparks and ash—across the festival grounds, past people trying to douse the burning thatch on a cottage, up and down twisting streets, and finally right to the center of town.

That was where the trail seemed to end. Astrid skidded to a stop at the edge of the square. It was paved with stone, so nothing was on fire, although a few wisps of smoke hinted that the Nix may have passed that way. However, the fountain and its marble horse stood as silent as ever, and nobody was in the square to point the way.

Panting, Astrid surveyed the businesses that lined the square. The grocer's shop, the post office, Mr. Smithin's forge, the Clydesdale Café . . . none showed any sign that the fiery visitor had passed through.

"Now what?" she muttered to Cork, who was riding in her shirt pocket as usual. He let out an uncertain chirp in response.

Astrid became aware that people were shouting somewhere behind her. Realizing that there must still be fires burning in the Nix's wake, she turned and hurried back to help put them out.

"That's the last of 'em!" someone called out, as one of the cetacequines who lived in the nearby Fastalon River spurted a great gush of water out through his blowhole, dousing the last of the fires started by the Nix.

"Whew!" Astrid wiped her sooty brow. "Thank goodness." She glanced down to check on Cork, who was also smudged with ash but otherwise fine.

When she looked up again, she

found herself the object of stares. The other townspeople who had fought the fires were already wondering aloud at the existence of the Nix. More than one of them had heard about the fire in the Sundlos' kitchen and had soon put two and two together, noting that the Nix seemed to turn up only when Astrid was about.

"Did you do something to provoke the beast, Astrid?" Mr. Brissl, the town's head custodian, peered at her with his small gray eyes.

"No!" Astrid protested. She paused, uncertain. "At least I don't think so. . . ."

She was interrupted by a general gasp and murmur. Turning, she saw Fiona pacing majestically toward her, her fiery red coat dimming the memory of the flames.

That took the attention off Astrid. Fiona stood for a moment, allowing the townspeople to gawk and admire as they pleased. Then she bowed her head, sending the image of Astrid riding. Astrid was thrilled to accept the invitation. She climbed aboard, and Fiona headed across the fields toward the Olav estate.

Astrid was about to ask Fiona if she knew anything about the Nix when she felt a slight hitch in the mare's gait. That reminded her that she'd meant to see if Mr. Smithin could help Fiona.

She said as much to the mare. "What do you think?" she asked, not sure how the legendary horse might react to such a suggestion. "Mr. Smithin really is a very good blacksmith. If anyone can figure out how to help you, it's him."

Astrid felt herself wrapped in a glow of agreement and thanks. She smiled and slid down from the mare's back, not wanting to stress Fiona's bad foot any more than necessary, and the two of them turned and walked back toward town and the forge.

"It's an honor, Fiona," Mr. Smithin

said with a polite bow, when Astrid introduced them. He bent toward her left front leg. "May I?"

Fiona lifted her hoof as he reached for it.

"Well, here's our trouble," he said at once. "The end of this shoe is bent!"

"Can you fix it?" Astrid asked, peering past him at the mangled horseshoe.

The blacksmith studied it for another moment and then shook his head. "I'm afraid not," he said, running his soot-blackened fingers around the rim. "These shoes are made of durium. My tools aren't strong enough, nor can my forge burn hot enough to shape that metal."

"Durium?" Astrid echoed. "I found a set of durium tools. Would that help?"

Mr. Smithin looked surprised. "Durium tools? Really?" he said. "I suppose it's worth a try. I still might not be able to reshape the shoe without a hotter

fire. But with those tools, at least I could remove it. That would have to be more comfortable for you, yes?" He looked at Fiona, who bent her head in assent.

"I'll be right back!" Astrid cried, already turning to race for home.

When she returned with the old tools, she found that Mr. Smithin had set out a bucket of fresh water for Fiona. Cork had stayed behind as well and was perched on the blacksmith's battered iron hoof-rest, enjoying a crumb he'd found somewhere.

"Here they are," Astrid panted, skidding to a stop in front of the forge. She pulled back the leather to reveal the ancient tools.

"Interesting!" Mr. Smithin reached for the hammer.

Before he could grasp it, there was a loud crackle and spit as the forge's iron door flew open. Astrid screamed as ̲ ̲ ̲ll, blazing figure leaped out of the ̲ ̲ ̲ ̲ht at her!

9

Astrid ducked just in time. A searing wave of heat struck her as the Nix flew past her. Spinning around, she saw the creature skitter to a stop, leaving sparks in his wake, and turn toward the durium tools. He stared at them with glittering black eyes and let out a small, triumphant cry.

He's after my tools! she realized. She couldn't imagine why, but she knew she had to keep them from the Nix if Mr. Smithin was to help Fiona. She grabbed the tools and raced out of the shop, heading straight for the horse fountain in the center of the square. She didn't look back until she was submerged in the cool spring water, only the top of her head above the surface.

The Nix was spinning furiously in the forge's wide courtyard, sending out sparks and puffs of smoke in every direction. He crashed into the gate and bounced off, and then banged into the forge itself, knocking it to the ground with a clatter. Cork let out a squeal of terror and leaped up onto Fiona's withers, where he clung to her mane.

"Begone, you!" Mr. Smithin shouted, grabbing the bucket of water and slinging it at the Nix.

There was splash, a sizzle, and a high-pitched squeal of dismay. A great dark puff of smoke enveloped the forge. Astrid blinked, unable to see what was happening for a few seconds.

When the smoke cleared, there

was no sign of the Nix. Mr. Smithin was heaving the forge back upright with assistance from Fiona, although Astrid could see that its fire was out. The rest of the courtyard was a mess—ash, tools, and debris everywhere.

She climbed out of the fountain and hurried to help set things right. "I think he was after my tools," she told Mr. Smithin.

He nodded grimly. "That would explain why he's been following you about." Glancing around his shop, he sighed. "It seems he'll stop at nothing to get what he wants."

Astrid's eyes filled with tears as she realized he was right. She'd brought the Nix here; this was her fault. So were all the fires and damage from earlier. The townspeople had been right to glare and whisper.

"I should go," she said. "Far away from here. Maybe to Granddad's cabin—he's so wise. He might be able to help me figure out how to banish the Nix once and for all."

"You may be right," Mr. Smithin agreed. "You'd best leave now, before that thing comes back. Don't worry, I'll let your parents know where you've gone and why." He glanced at Fiona. "Will you take her up the mountain, Fiona? I know she'll be safe with you."

Fiona whinnied in response.

"First, Mr. Smithin, can you remove that shoe?" Astrid asked the blacksmith. "I don't want her to have to carry me so far when she's in pain."

"Of course." Mr. Smithin carefully unwrapped the waterlogged leather containing the durium tools. "As I said, though, all I can do is remove it. I'm afraid your gait will still be uneven, Fiona. Perhaps once Astrid is safe you can travel to the fiery slopes of Lava Mountain on the other side of Darkcomb Forest, where you should be able to find a fire hot enough to repair the bent durium."

Astrid hated to think of Fiona ever leaving, especially to travel so far, although she knew it was important that the shoe get fixed. "Thank you," she said, watching as Mr. Smithin selected a tool and then bent over Fiona's hoof. He rested it on his thighs as he worked the nails and clinches loose and finally pulled the shoe free. It fell to the floor with a clatter, its weight cracking one of the cobblestones.

"There you are." Mr. Smithin set Fiona's bare hoof back down and then straightened up. "It's the best I can do. I hope it helps."

It was dark by the time Astrid, Cork, and Fiona arrived at Nikolas Sundlo's cabin. Astrid had spent the last few minutes of the journey trying to keep from falling asleep right there on the mare's back. Not only was she exhausted after the long day, but Fiona's gallop was so smooth and rhythmic that it felt like being rocked in a cradle. The occasional hitch in stride was much reduced, although Astrid now knew the mare well enough to feel that she was still favoring the bare hoof slightly.

Once the Nix is gone, I'll help her figure out how to fix that shoe, she thought sleepily. *It's the least I can do for her. . . .*

Fiona leaped gracefully across the little stream in front of the cabin, landing lightly in the front yard. Astrid slid down from her back, being careful not to crush Cork, who was snoring softly in her pocket. Paal had been dozing in the shelter of the cabin's overhang when they arrived. He lifted his head in surprise and let out a wheezy neigh, bringing Astrid's grandfather hurrying out with a lantern.

"Astrid!" Nikolas ran to hug her. "Is something wrong? The family—"

"Don't worry, everyone's fine," Astrid said. She went on to tell him the whole story. Her grandfather listened carefully, welcoming Fiona and assuring Astrid that they would come up with a plan in the morning.

"But for now, I can tell you're all exhausted," he said. "Off to bed. Everything will seem brighter after a good night's sleep."

"Ouch!" Astrid came suddenly out of a dream to find Cork yanking at her hair. "Cork, what is it? You woke me up!" The mouse chittered frantically, jumping up and down and pointing off into the darkness. Astrid sat up in her bed, rubbing her head.

Two glowing red eyes blinked into view, staring straight at her. The Nix!

Grabbing the candlestick beside her bed, she swung it at the Nix. There was a thud and a squeal, and the creature went flying—right out the open window!

"I'm done being chased by you!" Astrid shouted, leaping out of bed and

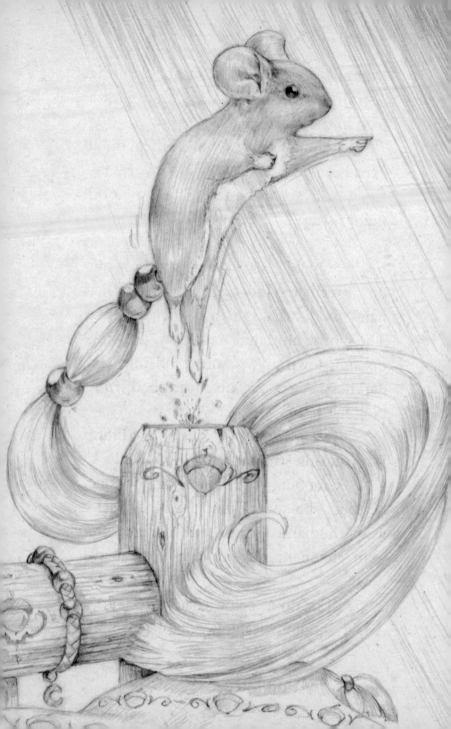

racing for the door. By the time she got outside, the Nix had jumped to his feet and was running across the yard, flames flying back from his head and hands.

The fiery creature glanced over his shoulder. His glowing eyes widened—and then he tripped over a stone and went flying right into the mountain stream that bisected the yard. There was a splash and a sizzle, and then silence.

Skidding to a stop at the edge of the stream, Astrid gasped. It was too dark and the water was moving too fast for her to see much, but the small black shape at the bottom of the stream wasn't moving. She put a hand to her mouth.

Did I . . . did I just kill *the Nix?*

CHAPTER

10

A loud whinny broke the still night air, followed by the sound of galloping hooves. Fiona burst into view, heading straight for the stream. As Astrid watched in surprise, the mare fished a little black thing out of the cold water with her teeth. It looked like a lump of coal—a shivering lump with chattering teeth.

"C-c-c-cold!" it said in a raspy, tinny little voice.

"You can talk!" Astrid blinked in amazement. *This* was the dreaded Nix?

This shivering, helpless little black figure with big sad eyes and a hoarse voice like a feathered jewel frog?

Then another set of thoughts pulsed into her mind, and she realized Fiona was sending them. They were images of the Nix, happy and smiling in some dark, fiery, underground world. The Nix peeping out curiously through an immense stone door carved with images of horses. The Nix crying molten tears as he beat on that same door, which was now sealed—with him on the outside.

"Oh." Astrid stared at the pathetic, sopping-wet little creature standing there steaming gently in the moonlight. "So let me get this straight. You're telling me the Nix is just a fire creature who's been trying to return to his home under the earth? But all those stories everyone tells to scare children—all those fires . . ."

"Me sorry to scare everyone and cause trouble, miss," the Nix said in his raspy voice. He heaved a watery sigh that emitted a small puff of steam. "Me lost on surface for thousand years. Me cut off from home when me wandered through big door in mountain." He shrugged his thin, sooty shoulders. "Me come back, find it shut and sealed. Since then, me try to stay warm to survive by hiding in fires. All the time me try to figure out how to go home."

"That's so sad!" Astrid exclaimed, trying to imagine being cut off from her home for one thousand years. "But if you're just trying to get home, why were you following me?"

"Me lived in blacksmith's forge for long time. But then he go away, and forge go cold." He shivered. "Me cannot live more than few hours with no fire, so me look for another good one. Me find it in your kitchen."

Astrid's eyes widened. Now she started to remember the comments— Mr. Smithin remarking on how his fire had been hard to get hot enough after his vacation; her mother's complaints about having to adjust her baking times recently. It was the Nix all along!

"All along, me no want to stay and be trouble. Me try to open door." He let out a watery sigh. "But it never open. And then big earthquake come, and door get lost. So me cannot even try anymore."

"Earthquake?" Astrid echoed.

Fiona sent another picture to her. This time it was of Mount Whitemantle shuddering as the chasm that would later become Bookend Pass split open.

"Are you talking about the Great Aurora Quake?" Astrid said uncertainly. "I've heard the legends, of course. It's said the mountain shook so hard that the stone statues of Bella and Bello appeared to rear and buck. But that must have happened—oh, three hundred years ago, at least!"

"Me give up after door disappear into mountain." The Nix sighed again.

"Me just try to stay warm. But then me hear you talk about tools. And door. And me wonder if it is same door and if tools carved that door!" Sparks flew from his head and hands as he smiled. "Me think if me get tools, me can find door and open it!"

"The door . . ." Astrid thought about the carved stone door she had found. It certainly looked as if it may have stood there for one thousand years. She stared at the Nix thoughtfully. Now that she was getting to know him, he didn't seem scary at all. He was just a sad, lonely little fellow who was desperate to get home.

"I think you may be right," she said. "Come inside and get warm in Granddad's fire, and we'll check it out first thing in the morning—but only if you promise not to burn anything down in the meantime!"

"Me promise!" The Nix capered joyfully, more sparks shooting out from his body. One landed on a pile of dried leaves and set it alight. Fiona stomped it out before the fire could spread. The Nix grinned sheepishly. "That is, me *try*."

"That it!" the Nix cried, dancing vigorously. "Door to me home!"

Astrid, the Nix, and Cork were standing in front of the carved door Astrid had found only days before. The three of them had traveled down the mountain first thing that morning. The durium tools were in a bag slung over Astrid's shoulder.

"Great," she said. "Now we just have to figure out how to get it open."

Pulling out the durium hammer and chisel from her bag, she placed the chisel in the seam of the doorway and swung the hammer.

ZZZZZZZT! The sound of metal striking metal was lost in a clap of thunder and a blinding blue flash of light. Astrid was thrown backward, her hands stinging. Cork hid in terror inside her collar, his teeth chattering.

When the blue light faded, Astrid saw the hammer and chisel lying on the ground before the door, which stood as impassive as ever. The hammer's handle was cracked, and the chisel had broken completely in two.

"Oh, no!" she exclaimed, sitting up and crawling toward the tools.

"Foolish child!" a woman's voice rang out, strong and full of authority. "The magic that protects this place is even stronger than the stonemason's tools. The very tools that carved these great watchers have been destroyed because of you."

A woman was standing there before the door, tall and with hair like glossy raven feathers. Her dark locks appeared to be flowing in a breeze, even though the air where Astrid sat was still. The woman wore silver armor

and carried a massive shield and a silver-tipped spear. All around her horses suddenly appeared—horses such as Astrid had never seen, thousands of horses. She couldn't imagine how the hollow was large enough to hold them all, and yet there they were, snorting and stamping their feet. She wasn't sure whether to be thrilled to find herself in the presence of so many wonderful horses or frightened by the stern look of the Valkyrie—for Astrid knew the woman could only be a Valkyrie.

"Astrid," the woman spoke again. "Do you know what you have done?"

"N-n-no?" Astrid stammered. "Er, ma'am," she added quickly.

The woman's stern expression softened slightly. "No," she said. "I can see that you meant no harm. But this is a sacred spot. There are very few places in North of North that are forbidden, but this is one of them—and with good reason. Do you understand?"

Astrid had no idea what to say. She merely stared wide-eyed at the woman and the horses surrounding her.

"You do not." This time, the woman almost smiled. "That is just as well. You see, only members of the Rolanddotter family may enter here. This is their place. You do understand that you should not be here, do you not?"

"I—I do now," Astrid said. "Please, I meant no disrespect. I was only trying—"

"Then all is well," the tall woman interrupted her. "You have done no permanent harm. Remember what I have said and leave this place to its ghosts and memories."

"But—" Astrid said quickly. She had to explain about the Nix! Her voice was lost in the crack of a thunderclap. Even as she watched, the black-haired woman and the vast herd of horses seemed to shimmer as if seen through a thick mist.

And then the hollow was empty, except for her and her friends.

"Please don't cry," Astrid said to the Nix, as they trudged up the mountain again. "I'll come up with another plan. I promise." Still, her heart hurt for her new friend. Now that they were banished from the doorway, how were they ever going to get him home?

When they reached the cabin, Fiona was waiting. As soon as she saw her, Astrid raced forward and hugged her, burying her face in the mare's silky mane. She felt the warmth of Fiona's love surrounding her.

That made her feel a little better about the situation. Astrid could come up with another plan if she tried hard enough.

As that thought entered her mind, she felt Fiona's approval. She also received an image of the whole group traveling back down the mountain to Mr. Smithin's forge.

"Come on," she told Cork and the Nix. She didn't know what Fiona had in mind, but she trusted the mare's judgment. "Fiona wants us to head back to Canter Hollow."

Bidding farewell to Nikolas, Astrid and Cork rode down the mountain, the Nix scampering beside them. As soon as they reached the valley, Astrid asked Fiona to stop.

"We'd better leave the Nix hidden here," she said, glancing around the rocky field they were crossing. "I don't think the townsfolk will want to see him again."

But Fiona kept trotting without slowing her pace. Astrid could feel her disagreement.

"Are you sure?" Astrid said. "But all the damage from the fires . . ."

Still the mare kept trotting. Astrid wasn't sure why Fiona was so determined to keep the Nix with them. But she decided she would have to trust the mare's wisdom.

It was another hot summer day, and the streets were almost empty. The only people in view when they entered the village were a pair of little girls playing with a miniature horse with emerald-colored wings.

"Look! It's Fiona!" the elder girl exclaimed, clapping her hands.

The younger girl's eyes widened when she spotted the Nix in Fiona's shadow. "Isn't that—?" she cried.

But Fiona put on an extra burst of speed, rounding the corner into the town square before the girl could finish.

Mr. Smithin was at work at his forge shaping a hoop for a barrel, but he dropped his tools when he saw them— and the Nix.

"It's the rascal that nearly wrecked my shop!" he burst out angrily.

"Wait!" Astrid slid down from Fiona's back. "Please don't be angry with him, Mr. Smithin. Let us explain. . . ."

By the time she and Nix finished their story, the blacksmith's eyes were wide with wonder. "Well, now," he said, peering down at the sooty little creature. "I suppose we can let bygones be bygones." He took a deep breath and smiled, although he still looked a bit wary. "Any friend of Astrid's is a friend of mine."

Fiona nickered. With that, an image formed in all their minds of Mr. Smithin repairing Astrid's tools and using them to fix her horseshoe.

"But I can't repair durium metal, whether these tools or your shoe," he reminded the horse. "My fire won't burn hot enough."

Fiona tossed her head so that her mane flew around her neck. With that, they all received another image: the forge, and inside it the fiery little figure of the Nix!

"Of course!" Astrid cried, finally understanding. "The Nix made your forge burn hotter before, and he can do it again. I bet he can make it the hottest fire ever! That should be enough to repair the tools."

Mr. Smithin rubbed his chin, glancing from the Nix to the scorch marks that still remained on the cobblestones and walls from the creature's last visit. "I suppose it's worth a try," he agreed at last. "In you go, little fellow. But be careful!"

"Me be careful!" the Nix cried with delight. "You have best fire on surface world!" He scurried over and dived straight into the heart of the forge.

Astrid pumped the bellows as the Nix danced within the flames. Soon the fire was so hot that the cast-iron exterior of the forge started to smoke and melt.

"It can't take much more!" Mr. Smithin shouted over the sound of the crackling flames. "I'll have to hurry!"

Within minutes the tools were fixed and cooling in a bucket of water. Then the smith reached for the bent shoe, which he'd hung on a hook on the wall.

Astrid kept one nervous eye on the forge, fearing it might burst into a thousand fiery pieces at any moment. Sweat poured from Mr. Smithin's brow as he plunged the horseshoe into the fire using the durium tongs. When he pulled it out, it wasn't red-hot as Astrid had seen before, or even white-hot. It was *blue*-hot.

He set it on his anvil, which instantly began to smoke and melt, and lifted the durium hammer. Metal met metal with a resounding clang.

"Is it working?" she cried over the echoes.

"It is!" Mr. Smithin called back. He hammered the shoe expertly until the bent edge returned to its normal shape. Next he did the same with the horseshoe nails, first softening them in the blazing-hot fire and then straightening them by pounding with the durium hammer.

"All right!" he called to the Nix. "That's enough. Now get out of there before my forge explodes!"

The Nix popped out of the forge, and the fire immediately died back to its normal level. "So warm, so warm!" the Nix chanted happily, dancing around and leaving footprints in the dirt that each flamed briefly before collapsing into soot and ash. "Warmest me been since a thousand years! Thank you, friends!"

"You're welcome," Astrid said with a smile. She watched as Mr. Smithin lifted

Fiona's hoof, checked the shoe to be sure it had cooled and that he'd shaped it correctly, and then carefully nailed it back into place with the durium hammer.

Astrid's mind was already shifting to what lay ahead. How in the world were they supposed to help the Nix return home?

Fiona stamped her hoof as if to test her new shoe, sending up sparks from the stones underfoot. In her mind, Astrid found an image of the glade with the standing stones where she'd met Philenia. She understood the horse's meaning immediately. They had to go back there. She understood that Fiona had always known that this was the answer to the Nix's problem.

Why didn't she tell us sooner? Astrid wondered. *What was she waiting for? Was she distracted by her sore hoof?*

But she decided it didn't matter. She trusted her new friend, and that was enough.

* * *

As they stepped into the glade, Fiona stopped. Dismounting, Astrid glanced around. The little valley looked much as she remembered, aside from the absence of the rainstorm and Philenia's camp.

"Now what?" the Nix asked, peering around. "Me no see door here."

Fiona suddenly reared and trumpeted fiercely. Astrid and her friends watched as the red mare began to trot in a circle around the standing stones where Philenia's campfire had been. Around and around she went, faster and faster, breaking first into a canter and then a gallop. Soon she was moving almost too fast to see, appearing as little more than a red streak. Sparks began to fly from her metal-shod hooves.

Astrid understood without being told that there was magic at work here— magic that she guessed would not have been possible had the mare's shoe not been fixed, for Fiona was moving as Astrid had never seen her move before.

Meanwhile, the Nix was drifting forward, drawn toward the shower of sparks. The tiny bits of fire began to find him, landing on his sooty skin and setting him alight. Soon flames crackled atop his head and from his feet and fingertips.

"Warm!" he cried. "Me warm!"

Fiona galloped even faster, throwing up more sparks toward the Nix. As Astrid and Cork watched in amazement, the Nix burned brighter and hotter.

Then he began to grow!

He swelled from the size of a pizzazzupine to that of a whiffle bear in minutes. Soon he was as tall as Astrid and then taller than Fiona. And still he kept growing, up and up, until he was as tall as the clock tower in Canter Hollow.

"Warm!" he shouted again, his voice now as deep as thunder with the sizzle of lightning around its edges.

"Me going home!"

Reaching down from his great height, he grabbed the durium hammer, which looked comically small in his huge, flaming hand. He struck the ground with it. There was a sound like an immense thunderclap, and the earth cracked open, hot lava pouring out.

Astrid grabbed Cork and jumped up on a nearby boulder for safety, although she soon saw that the molten magma was being contained by the standing stones, splashing up against their craggy surfaces but going no farther. The lava swirled and parted, revealing a fiery tunnel below the earth's surface.

"Good-bye, Astrid!" the Nix called. "Thank you, me friend!"

"Good-bye! I'll miss you!" Astrid called back, as the Nix dived into the magma. He vanished immediately, the hole closing behind him.

At long last, the Nix was going home!

When an exhausted Astrid rode into Canter Hollow with Cork on her shoulder, she found the entire village gathered to meet them. From the exclamations of surprise and joy, she soon deduced that everyone there had heard the thunderclaps and seen the smoke and ash pouring down from the mountain. When Mr. Smithin had told them what he knew, all had feared the worst.

Astrid jumped down from Fiona's back and quickly explained what had happened. She had feared that the townspeople might be angry with her for helping the Nix. However, she soon realized that it was quite the contrary—they hailed her as a hero! She was hoisted onto Mr. Smithin's shoulders, no one seeming to mind or even notice that she was covered in soot and grime as they carried her about the town square singing and cheering. Even her brothers joined in.

"That's my sister!" she heard Kimo exclaiming proudly. "I taught her everything she knows."

Finally Astrid convinced them to put her down. Marta Cavinol, the tall, raven-haired mayor of Canter Hollow, approached her. "Pardon my intrusion into your celebration, Astrid. But I must ask you, what has become of the lava?" the mayor inquired with concern. "Will we need to erect a warning sign for travelers?"

Astrid shook her head. "The tunnel closed while we watched, and the lava drained away. All that's left to mark the spot is a trickle of water and steam from the rock—it seems to be forming a new hot spring."

"Please, everyone." Astrid's mother pushed her way through the crowd. "I must take my daughter home now. She needs a rest after all she's been through."

It took a bit more than that to convince Astrid's new fans to let her go. But eventually she found herself walking back toward their house with Fiona striding in front of them.

When they reached the yard, the great red mare turned and gazed at Astrid with somber dark eyes. An image formed in Astrid's mind—one of Fiona galloping away. Astrid's eyes filled with tears as she realized what the horse was telling her— it was time for her to go.

"Oh, but I'll miss you so much!" Astrid cried, flinging her arms around Fiona's neck and twisting her silken mane between her fingers. "I can't believe you have to leave!"

The horse nuzzled the back of her neck, saying good-bye. Tears flowed freely down Astrid's cheeks, but beneath it all she felt a sort of humble joy settle into her, for she knew in her heart that she and Fiona would always be friends and that they would surely meet again someday.

"Farewell for now, then," Astrid whispered, planting a kiss on the mare's soft nose. Then she stood back, stroking Cork's fur, and watched as Fiona galloped out of sight.

"What is it, Cork?" Astrid asked, glancing up from her task of peeling potatoes for supper.

Several days had passed since her adventure, and the Sundlo household had mostly settled back into its usual rhythms. But now Cork was dancing and chirping, seeming excited about something.

Astrid stood and followed him toward the door. When she looked outside, she saw a tube-shaped package leaning against the doorframe.

"What's this?" she exclaimed in surprise. Picking it up, she saw her name written on it in big, loopy script.

She pulled off the brown paper and found a leather tube within. Inside that was a rolled-up piece of thick, creamy paper.

Astrid unrolled it and spread it out on the kitchen table. It was a drawing—of *her*! It showed her and Cork watching as Fiona created sparks from her galloping hooves, the Nix growing within the resulting blaze.

"Oh, it's incredible!" she murmured to Cork, who had climbed up the table leg to peer at the drawing.

He chirped and pointed to a corner of the paper. Astrid saw a signature there, written in the same bold, loopy hand as

her name had been on the package. She smiled when she saw the signature: *Philenia True.*

Thank you, she thought, hoping that somehow her gratitude would reach the artist. She knew that this drawing would hold a place of honor on her wall among her own sketches. It would be a beautiful memento of her new friends Cork and the Nix, and of her exciting adventure with her magical, legendary, wonderful friend Fiona—a reminder that sometimes dreams can come true.

"And that," Joani said in conclusion, "is the story of Sigga." She looked at each of her children in turn. "Remember this, Sevi and Cody: Choices do matter. Sigga's choice had consequences that lasted the rest of her life and a thousand years beyond it."

Sevi sat in silence for a moment. *Sigga's choice was kind of like mine is,* she thought. *Choose one path, and help many people. Choose the other, and help one person you love. How do you decide something like that?*

"Do you think Sigga did the wrong thing, Mama?" she asked.

"That's a difficult question," answered Joani. "I admire Sigga's bravery in choosing to follow her heart. And she did save Archer's life. But she paid a heavy price, and you could also argue that North of North paid a price, too, in losing her. On the other hand, although our world is not perfect, it is a wonderful place the way it is. I think that you will have to make up your own mind about whether or not you think Sigga did the wrong thing."

"I wish Sara's horses were still around in North of North," Cody said, jumping up and galloping around the edge of the room.

"They are," Joani replied. "Or at least, their descendants are. And it's said that the four legendary horses Jewel, Fiona, Nike, and Thunder still roam the land. Sara and Sigga chose them to help protect North of North, you know, and Sara made them immortal so they would always be able to come to the aid of those who most need their help."

"Sevi, don't you think it would be great to ride one of the legendary horses? Especially Thunder! I like him the best because he's a stallion. And he can make lightning come out of his hooves. Wouldn't it be great to ride him?"

"It would be pretty amazing," agreed Sevi. She'd always loved Thunder, too—the striking black stallion with the image of a lightning bolt seared on his flank. Thunder was born of a great storm, and he was said to share in the power of Nature itself. He seemed so strong, so sure of himself.

He'd know which path was right for me, Sevi thought. *If only Thunder could come tell me what to choose!*

Then she had to smile at her own foolishness. A great, legendary horse like Thunder had more important things to do than help a young girl make up her mind!

Go to
www.bellasara.com
and enter the webcode below.
Enjoy!

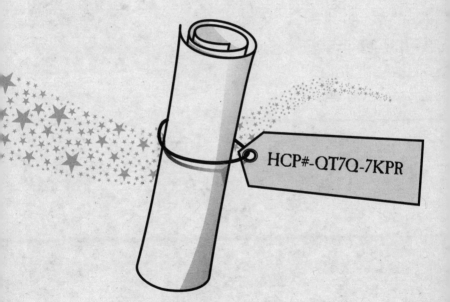

HCP#-QT7Q-7KPR